MORPHA

A RAIN FOREST STORY

story by
Michael Tennyson

illustrations by
Jennifer H. Yoswa

THE COLORADO MOUNTAIN CLUB PRESS
GOLDEN, CO

SCFD
Scientific & Cultural
Facilities District

Making It Possible.

PUBLISHED IN THE UNITED STATES BY:
The Colorado Mountain Club Press
710 10th Street #200
Golden, CO 80401
(303) 279 3080
Email: cmcpress@cmc.org
Website: www.cmc.org
*Founded in 1912, The Colorado Mountain Club
is a nonprofit recreation, outdoor education, and
conservation organization with over
10,000 members. We are organized:
"to unite the energy, interest, and knowledge of
the students and lovers of the mountains."*

Managing Editor: Terry Root
Layout Assistant: Steve Meyers
Proofing: June Barber and Linda Grey

THIS BOOK IS A PRODUCTION OF:
© 2002 The Butterfly Pavillion
6252 W. 104 Ave.
Westminster, CO 80020
(303) 469-5441
Website: www.butterflies.org
*The Butterfly Pavilion is an educational facility
for the study of invertebrates. The facility exists
to foster an appreciation of butterflies and other
invertebrates while reminding the public about
the need for conservation of threatened habitats
in the tropics and around the world.*

Project Director: Patrick Tennyson
Butterfly Pavilion President/CEO: Bob Bonacci
Butterfly Pavilion Science Advisory Team:
John Watts, Jill Graham, and Shirley Jamiel
Illustrations in Glossary and
Teacher's Help Page by: Deborah Brooks

FUNDING PROVIDED BY:
The Scientific and Cultural
Facilities District of greater
metropolitan Denver, CO
Website: www.scfd.org
*We gratefully acknowledge the
financial support of the citizens of
Colorado through the Scientific and
Cultural Facilities District for the
publication of this book.*

LIBRARY OF CONGRESS CATALOGING-IN-PUBLICATION DATA

Tennyson, Michael, 1959-
  Morpha : a rain forest story / by Michael Tennyson ; illustrated by
Jennifer H. Yoswa.
    p. cm.
Summary: Morpha, a Blue Morpho butterfly begins life in the rain forest
of Costa Rica and describes the interdependence of plants and animals.
  ISBN 0-9671466-8-2 (alk. paper)
  1. Morpho--Juvenile fiction. [1. Morpho--Fiction. 2.
Butterflies--Fiction. 3. Rain forest ecology--Fiction. 4.
Ecology--Fiction. 5. Costa Rica--Fiction.] I. Yoswa, Jennifer H., 1963- ,
ill. II. Title.
  PZ10.3.T262 Mo 2002
  [Fic]--dc21

                              2002007849

ABOUT THE AUTHOR
Michael Tennyson, a former natural resource manager,
lives with his wife in Lafayette, Colorado. He attended the
University of Colorado for undergraduate and graduate
studies. For ten months each year he teaches fifth graders
about ecology, environments, life cycles and food webs
along with reading, writing, and math. When not in the
classroom, he may be found writing, traveling, gardening,
hiking and floating backcountry haunts, or stalking trout
knee-deep in some Western river.
Morpha is his first published book.

ABOUT THE ILLUSTRATOR
Jennifer H. Yoswa has been an elementary teacher and
counselor in Aurora Public Schools for sixteen years. She
recently discovered a passion for art and is rarely seen
without paintbrush in hand. Jennifer lives in Centennial,
Colorado with her husband and two children.

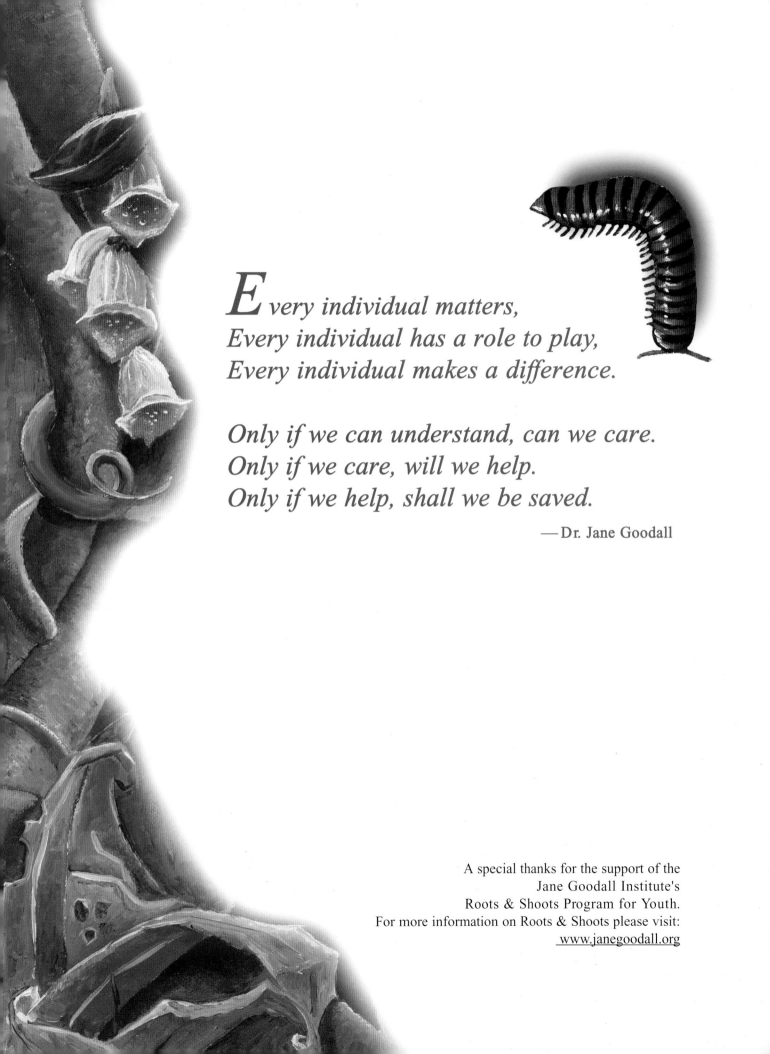

E very individual matters,
Every individual has a role to play,
Every individual makes a difference.

Only if we can understand, can we care.
Only if we care, will we help.
Only if we help, shall we be saved.

—Dr. Jane Goodall

A special thanks for the support of the
Jane Goodall Institute's
Roots & Shoots Program for Youth.
For more information on Roots & Shoots please visit:
www.janegoodall.org

It was like waking into a dream, only real. Morpha hung exhausted from a branch after wiggling free from her chrysalis. She had been waiting for this moment for so long.

She gazed back at her brand new, beautiful, blue wings. They shimmered like a rainbow in the soft morning light, slowly filling with fluid, expanding and forming.

No longer a fat, lumpy caterpillar, she was now an adult Blue Morpho butterfly!

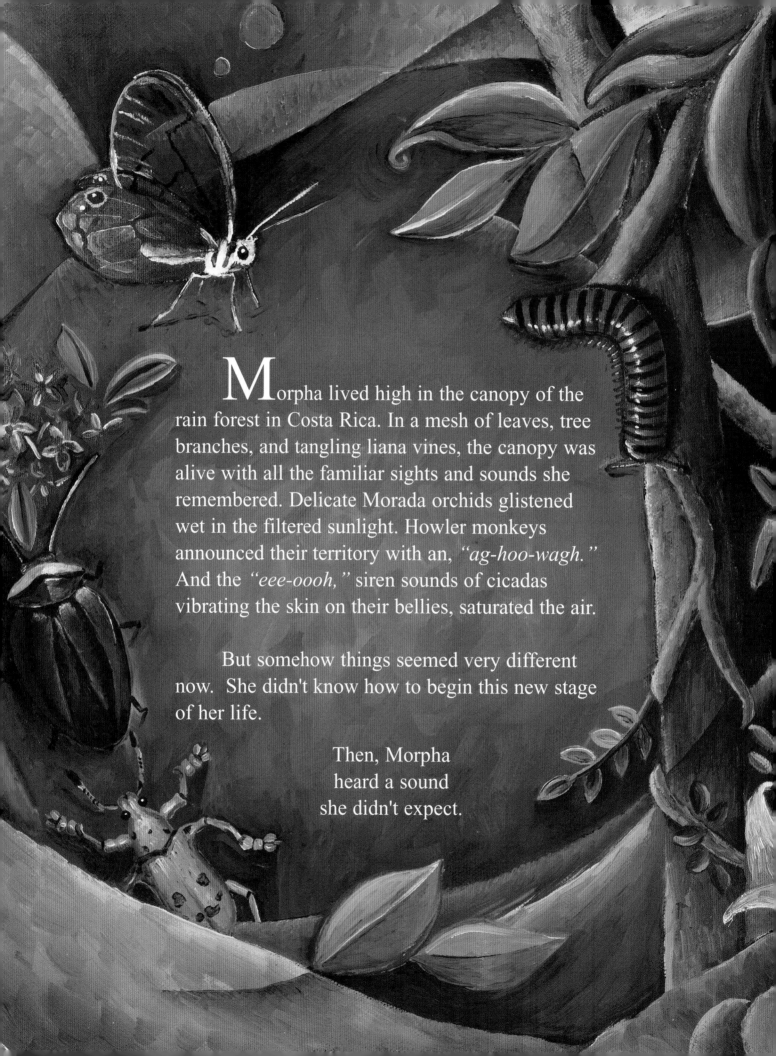

Morpha lived high in the canopy of the rain forest in Costa Rica. In a mesh of leaves, tree branches, and tangling liana vines, the canopy was alive with all the familiar sights and sounds she remembered. Delicate Morada orchids glistened wet in the filtered sunlight. Howler monkeys announced their territory with an, *"ag-hoo-wagh."* And the *"eee-oooh,"* siren sounds of cicadas vibrating the skin on their bellies, saturated the air.

But somehow things seemed very different now. She didn't know how to begin this new stage of her life.

Then, Morpha
heard a sound
she didn't expect.

"Hello little one,"

said a tender voice from above. Startled, Morpha looked up to see another large and pretty Morpho butterfly resting on a twig, just like herself.

"I didn't see you," Morpha said shyly.

"Well then, you have much to learn. A startled butterfly should never lie about with her brilliant, blue wings all spread out in the sun to be so easily seen," said the older, wiser butterfly.

Morpha was embarrassed. She was so proud of her new wings and slender black body. "I was just catching my breath and enjoying my new body."

"That's fine, of course, but to survive long enough to enjoy it, you must behave as a proper Morpho does, and learn about the rain forest. I am Azuela," she sighed, resting down again.

"Please Azuela, could you teach me?" Morpha said excitedly.

"Teach you?" Azuela said gently, "Why, I don't even know your name."

"Oh, excuse me, my name is Morpha, and I'm very pleased to meet you," Morpha said quickly.

"Well . . . I suppose your wings have warmed in the sun long enough to be ready for a flight. Follow me." Azuela launched into the air, flying gracefully upward.

Morpha tried her new wings. They really worked! With a dip, and a drop, she clumsily weaved up through woody vines, chasing Azuela high to the safety of a Cecropia tree.

Each moment, Morpha learned more from her new friend. She tried to eat the leaves of Mucuna vines, like she had when she was a caterpillar. But Azuela showed her how to find the delectable foods that all Morpho butterflies liked to eat. She taught Morpha how to sample soft fruit that had hung long on the trees and begun to decay. Never had she tasted anything so sweet and delicious!

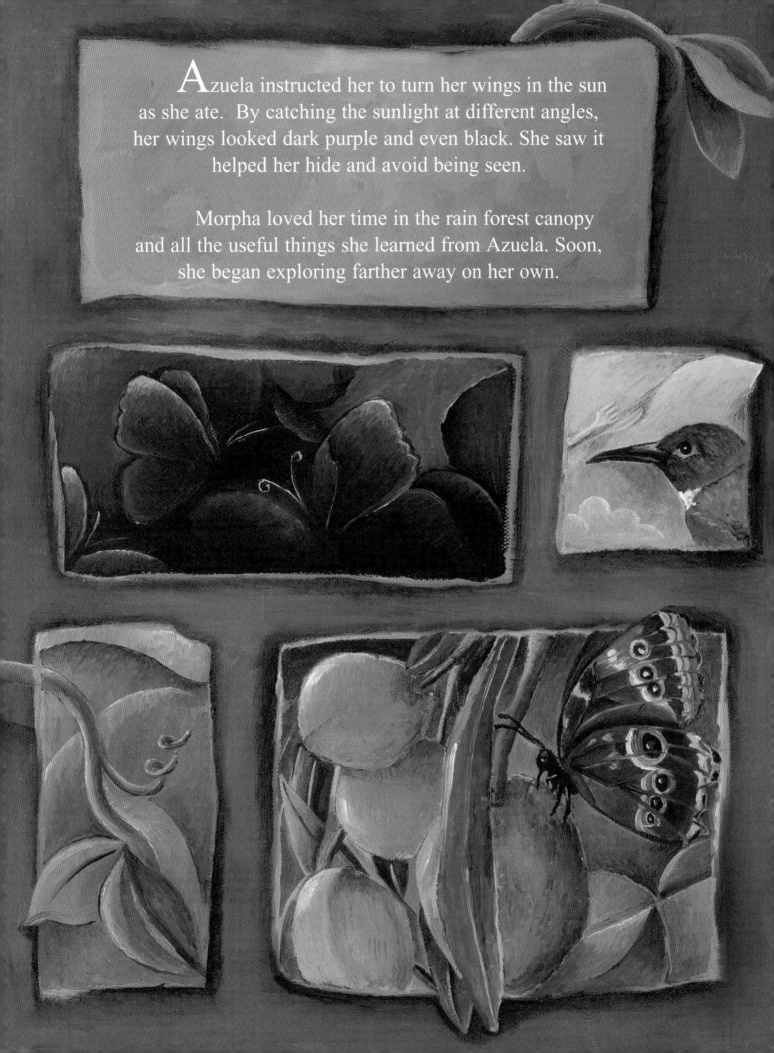

Azuela instructed her to turn her wings in the sun as she ate. By catching the sunlight at different angles, her wings looked dark purple and even black. She saw it helped her hide and avoid being seen.

Morpha loved her time in the rain forest canopy and all the useful things she learned from Azuela. Soon, she began exploring farther away on her own.

D elighted with her improving flying skills, Morpha flew higher than ever before. She flew even to where the treetops emerged into the open air. Here the sun shined brightly. The deep, azure sky seemed to stretch on forever.

While taking in this splendid view, a dazzling orange and green shape whizzed right by her. Looking down, she saw a bird change its direction and fly back hungrily toward her. Sensing danger, Morpha dashed for the safety of the trees.

In a flash, Azuela flew between her and the bird. The bird turned instantly, chasing Azuela instead. Morpha watched as Azuela began to zigzag,

up and down, and back and forth.

Every time the bird was about to snatch her out of midair, Azuela would change direction and the bird would miss.

Bit-by-bit

Azuela skittered her way back down into the treetops. The confused bird finally gave up and flew off.

Azuela landed beside Morpha, who was still gasping and shaking from the terrifying experience. "*W-what* was that?" sobbed Morpha.

"You're safe little one, for now," began Azuela calmly, soothing the frightened young butterfly. "You see Morpha, just as we need decaying fruit and other plants for food and shelter, Jacamar birds need butterflies to survive. But Jacamars and butterflies still live together in the rain forest. That is the natural way of life."

"There is a balance in the rainforest, little one. Energy for all living things comes from the sun high above and from within the water far below," Azuela continued. "In between is the living forest. Every plant and animal here are all part of a great cycle. Animals need the plants to survive, but the plants need the animals too. Eventually, all living things give their life's energy back to the forest. The cycle of life goes on. Everything has a part to play, and each thing depends on many others, helping the whole forest grow and thrive. In balance."

"The Jacamar does its part, just as we do. And you, little butterfly, must learn to avoid the dangers the forest holds. The wisest learn, and live longer."

"Like you," said Morpha piping in, "and that is just how I will be. There is just so much to learn and remember."

"You remember, and be careful Morpha. Every new event holds secrets for you to learn and someday pass on," Azuela finished, lovingly brushing Morpha's antennae with her own.

A moist, healthy fog always rose like clouds in the rain forest canopy. Azuela told Morpha this was part of the way the sun and water helped bring energy for life through the forest. And so much life! When the forest was chirping and buzzing with activity, Morpha, like all the animals, felt comfortable and peaceful.

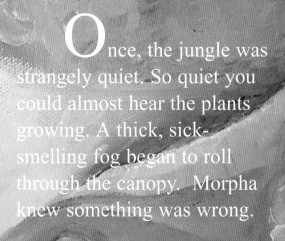

Once, the jungle was strangely quiet. So quiet you could almost hear the plants growing. A thick, sick-smelling fog began to roll through the canopy. Morpha knew something was wrong.

She worried, and went to Azuela. "That is the smell and sounds of Human animals in the forest," the elder butterfly told her. "Sometimes they make fires, and burn huge parts of the forest, leaving nothing behind but a black and barren wasteland where nothing would live on its own."

"But wise animals, like you little one, can feel changes in the forest, and know it is time to move on," said Azuela. With that, she flew slowly toward the huge leaves of a distant Kapok tree to wait for the danger to pass.

Morpha noticed Azuela's dull and tattered wings, and her aging, withering body. Sadly, Morpha knew she would soon have to fly the forest alone.

Morpha grew more at ease in her home and with her place in the balance of life in the rain forest. She worked hard to be ever wary of dangers.

She also tried to learn carefully from everything she saw while exploring new and different parts of the jungle, just as Azuela had taught her.

Fluttering down into the forest under story, she settled and stretched her proboscis into some lovely, rotting Mango fruit. A bustle of activity on a nearby Mucuna vine quickly caught Morpha's eye.

A crew of leaf cutter ants argued as they busied themselves, chewing out little round circles of Mucuna leaves.

"That's two done; you go girl!" said an ant, as a second ant began cutting away into another leaf circle with her jaws.

A third, smaller ant rushed up wagging its head, acting bossy. "I'm giving the orders today, Teri. Now you pick up one of those leaves and get in line!"

"Hold on, Grinda. I don't see you rushing your hairy legs back to the fungus farm!" said Teri, wagging right back.

"Don't even go there," Grinda said, "I'm in charge."

"Careful little sister, you'll get your antennae in a tangle. When Pinch's done, we can all go back together," scolded Teri.

Morpha could see many other ant teams cutting leaves and long lines of ants carrying away cut leaf discs. Suddenly, she remembered!

"Hey ladies! What's up?" said Morpha.

"Not now Blue, we're busy. And you should be too!" snapped Grinda.

"But it's me, Morpha, remember?"

"*Morf* who?" said Grinda, puzzled.

Just then, Pinch finished her last cut, and the third leaf disc fell on Grinda's head. "Poor little Grinda, so much to learn," said Pinch, "You know her! Remember the long, orange and red caterpillar that used to hang out underneath the Mucuna leaves with us? Hey, nice wings Morpha!"

"Sorry," said Grinda, rubbing her head, remembering. "I didn't mean to snap at you. Wow, you've changed!"

"Duh!" said Teri. "Just because Morpha's different, doesn't mean she isn't still important."

Pinch said, "Grinda, everything in the forest plays a special part. Ants use the Mucuna leaves — just like Morpha used to do."

Teri agreed quickly, "Yeah, only we grind up the leaves and use them to grow fungus for our food. And also like Morpha used to, we take only what we need, so the vine grows tall enough to reach the brighter sunlight of the canopy."

"Where it grows nectar-filled flowers for the bees' food," Pinch kept on before Grinda could get a single word out. "Then the bees pollinate the flowers, so that the flowers can make seed pods for animals like monkeys and tapir."

"Those bigger animals help scatter the seeds to make new Mucuna plants for us, caterpillars *and* ants. And that's just how it works for Mucuna plants," Teri finished. Grinda started to speak. Too late.

"The cycle goes around and around, like these leaf circles we cut," Pinch added, moving to pick up a leaf disc.

"There you go Grinda," Teri ended, pleased with herself. "Life in the forest."

"Well, it's great to see you again Morpha!" said Grinda finally, as Pinch and Teri started off with their leaves. "I . . .uh . . . guess we have to get going."

Speechless, Morpha watched the Atta Ant sisters march busily off with leaf cuttings held high in their jaws, and little Grinda racing to catch up with her big sisters. "Everything does have a part in it," she whispered, remembering Azuela's lesson about the cycle of forest life, "even caterpillars."

"That's right," said a low voice next to her.

"Even slugs."

Morpha jumped. Beside her, in a notch of the Mango tree, was a giant slug lying on a pile of dead leaves. It was a big, slimy blob of gray, narrower at one end, and flat along the bottom. The voice came from just below two round-ended, slimy eye stalks on the fatter end. She hadn't even noticed it lying there, silently blending in with the dead leaves.

"Ugh!

Morpha shivered. "What are *you*?"

"My name is Sylvester, thank you!" said the slug. "And I'm a slug of course. But don't worry. No one ever notices me, except for a few birds looking for a nice plump snack."

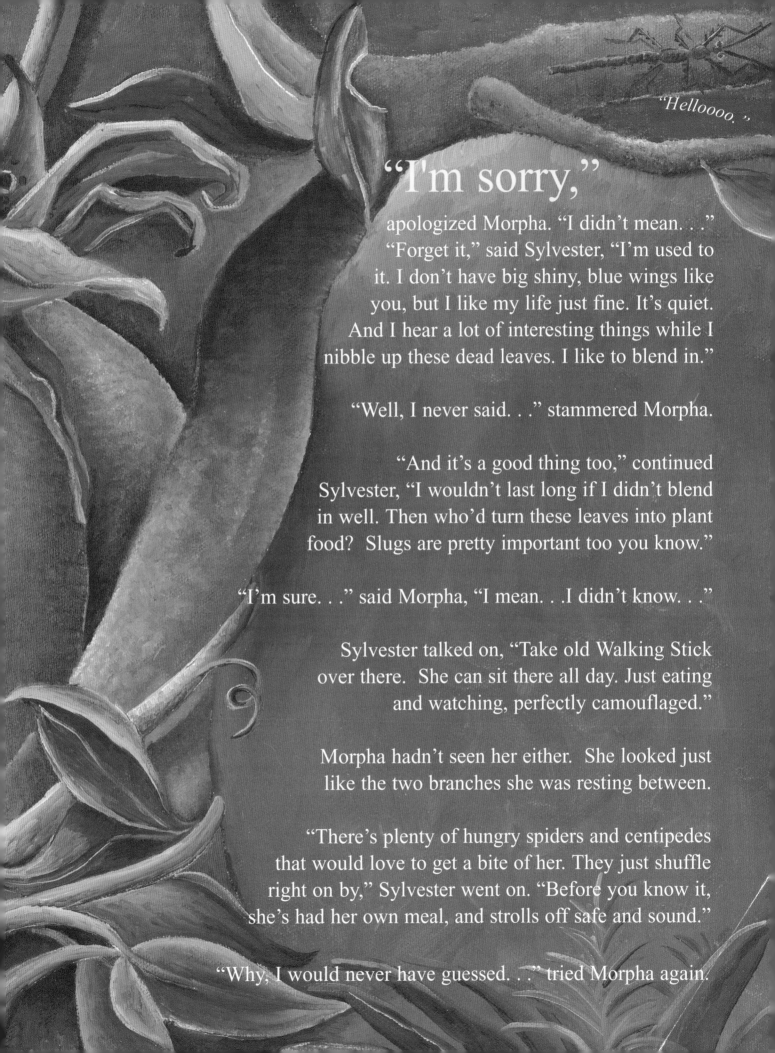

"Helloooo."

"I'm sorry,"

apologized Morpha. "I didn't mean. . ."

"Forget it," said Sylvester, "I'm used to it. I don't have big shiny, blue wings like you, but I like my life just fine. It's quiet. And I hear a lot of interesting things while I nibble up these dead leaves. I like to blend in."

"Well, I never said. . ." stammered Morpha.

"And it's a good thing too," continued Sylvester, "I wouldn't last long if I didn't blend in well. Then who'd turn these leaves into plant food? Slugs are pretty important too you know."

"I'm sure. . ." said Morpha, "I mean. . .I didn't know. . ."

Sylvester talked on, "Take old Walking Stick over there. She can sit there all day. Just eating and watching, perfectly camouflaged."

Morpha hadn't seen her either. She looked just like the two branches she was resting between.

"There's plenty of hungry spiders and centipedes that would love to get a bite of her. They just shuffle right on by," Sylvester went on. "Before you know it, she's had her own meal, and strolls off safe and sound."

"Why, I would never have guessed. . ." tried Morpha again.

"**Of course** you wouldn't, living up in the canopy," said Sylvester. "I'll bet you don't even know why the bottom side of your wings are brown with those spots that look like big eyes."

"I guess I never gave it much thought," said Morpha, flapping one glossy wing to have a look at the underside.

"Silly butterfly!" laughed Sylvester. "If you close your wings up while you eat, you look just like the ground. Or even, some of the animals that live there. Very handy for hiding down on the forest floor."

"I've never even been to the forest floor," Morpha exclaimed.

"Many animals never go down at all," said Sylvester. "But you really should try it sometime. A lot of fruit falls to the ground to decay, you know."

"Well. . .*maybe*. . ." said Morpha uncertainly.

"Rotten fruit, *hmmm*. . ." Sylvester wondered aloud. "Maybe I'll go myself."

"All animals and plants have important work to do in the forest — no matter what they look like," the Walking Stick finally spoke. "That's why we all have special talents, like blending in, so we can all get on with our business."

"Well thank you both," said Morpha gratefully. "I will remember, and I'll try to be a little more sensitive next time." Then Morpha flitted away from the Mango tree, on to new adventures.

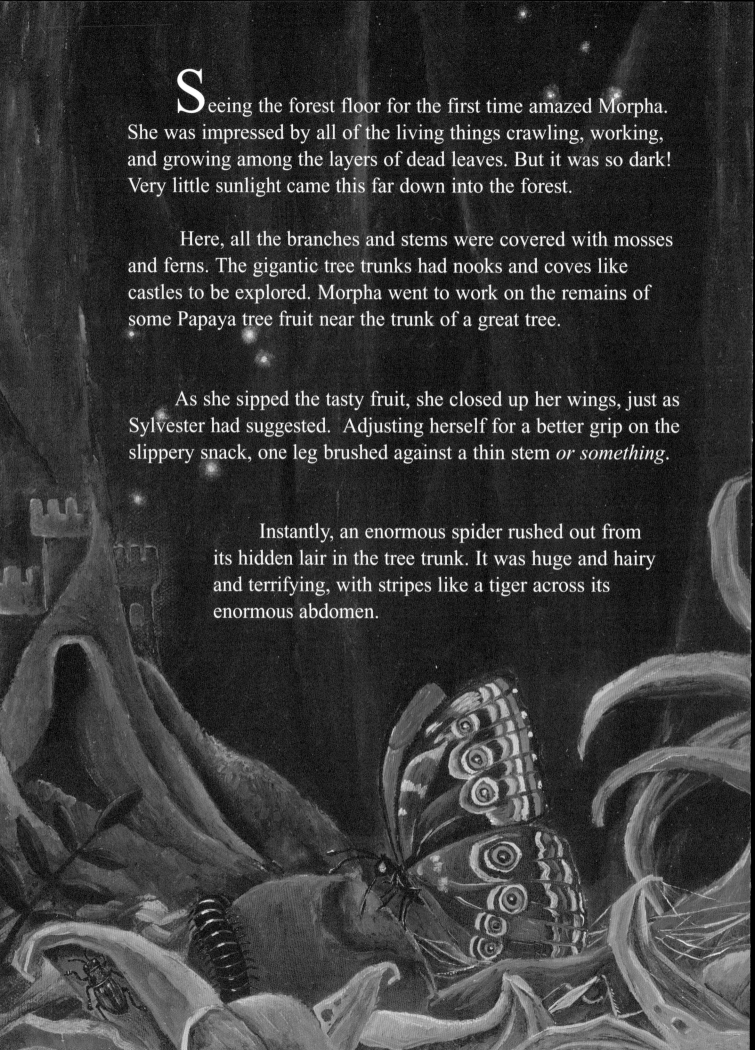

Seeing the forest floor for the first time amazed Morpha. She was impressed by all of the living things crawling, working, and growing among the layers of dead leaves. But it was so dark! Very little sunlight came this far down into the forest.

Here, all the branches and stems were covered with mosses and ferns. The gigantic tree trunks had nooks and coves like castles to be explored. Morpha went to work on the remains of some Papaya tree fruit near the trunk of a great tree.

As she sipped the tasty fruit, she closed up her wings, just as Sylvester had suggested. Adjusting herself for a better grip on the slippery snack, one leg brushed against a thin stem *or something*.

Instantly, an enormous spider rushed out from its hidden lair in the tree trunk. It was huge and hairy and terrifying, with stripes like a tiger across its enormous abdomen.

Before
Morpha
could
move,
the spider was upon her!

Then it stopped.

"Ahhhhh!" yelled the startled beast, rocking backward.

Morpha was stunned, frozen face to face with a huge Tarantula. Finding her own voice, she screamed back, *"Ahhhh!"* and launched into the air.

"A butterfly?" said the Spider confused.

"What did you expect?" said Morpha feeling safer, but still trying to catch her breath.

"You brushed that strand of web in front of my door," said the spider. *"Whew!* I thought you were a bird that had just tricked me into becoming supper."

"A bird?" puzzled Morpha. Then she remembered the eyespots on her wings, for camouflage. "It really does work," she said happily, landing on a fern above the spider's head. "Don't feel bad. I thought I had just made another blunder myself. I'm Morpha."

"They call me Tigerump," said the spider. "That's a pretty neat trick with the eye on the wing."

"So was that little silky doorbell you got me to step on," said Morpha.

Both of them laughed a moment, and then stopped. In the silence, they noticed how eerily quiet and smoky the forest had become, and instantly knew what it meant.

"Morpha, to be safe, you'd better come into my house." said Tigerump.

"I'm sure," replied Morpha. "Wouldn't you love to have a butterfly over for dinner?"

"Don't worry," he said, disappearing into his tree trunk cave. "You're not my type."

Morpha could feel there wasn't much time left. Warily, she followed him in.

Out of danger inside Tigerump's lair, the two became quick friends. Morpha thought the spider's eating habits were revolting. But she had learned not to judge others. All living things had an important job to do in the forest. Except, she thought, Humans.

"How *do* Humans fit into the cycle of the rain forest?" Morpha wondered aloud to the spider. "They don't seem to help the balance at all"

"In the forest's rich web of life, many things are a mystery," he answered. "I have seen some Humans that live in the forest right along with plants and animals. But others just don't belong. You know when they are coming, and life is never the same when they leave."

"Oh, I've been caught in their fire before," said Morpha coolly. "But it passed quickly, and the forest was still there."

"I think this time may be different Morpha. We will have a long wait before we can go out. As for the forest . . . we shall see."

When Tigerump and Morpha finally emerged from the tree trunk, the life they had known was gone. Gone were the lush, green layers of the forest with all its wonders. A blackened, smoking earth lay open to a hazy, gray sky. The moist, refreshing air had vanished. Only a dreary, deserted emptiness was left behind. Nothing could live here.

"We have to search for a new home," said Tigerump sadly. Morpha was astonished. "But where can we go and how will we live?" she said fearfully. "What will we eat?"

"That, we will have to discover," said Tigerump. "Let's go."

Following the debris-choked river, they set off in search of signs of their forest. Morpha trembled in the smoggy sky while Tigerump carefully trudged across the scorched ground. The burned out land seemed to extend on forever. They grew hungry and tired, and still found no trace of the forest.

From the air, Morpha could see a dust cloud rising in the distance. She could hear the strange rumbling sounds of Human machines. Turning around to warn her friend, she was surprised by a group of Humans running right toward her. Right between her and Tigerump!

"Morpha!" she heard Tigerump call out as she fainted, captured in a Human's net!

When Morpha awoke, she found herself in a place much like it was before the fire. Only a bad dream, she wondered? Morpha looked more carefully. She was suddenly very happy. All around her were the sights, sounds and smells of home. She was back in the forest — *almost.*

"Morpha!" said a familiar voice from below her.

"Who. . ." said Morpha, looking down surprised.

"I thought that might be you," said the voice again. It seemed to come from a pile of dead leaves on the opposite side of some type of mesh barrier.

"Sylvester!" cried Morpha. "But how. . ."

"Oh, I've been here a while," said the slug. "I thought I'd drowned, falling into the river during that horrible fire. But I washed up on shore, just over there." He pointed with a bend of one slimy antenna.

"It's so good to see you!" cried Morpha again.
"It wasn't a dream then. It was. . ."

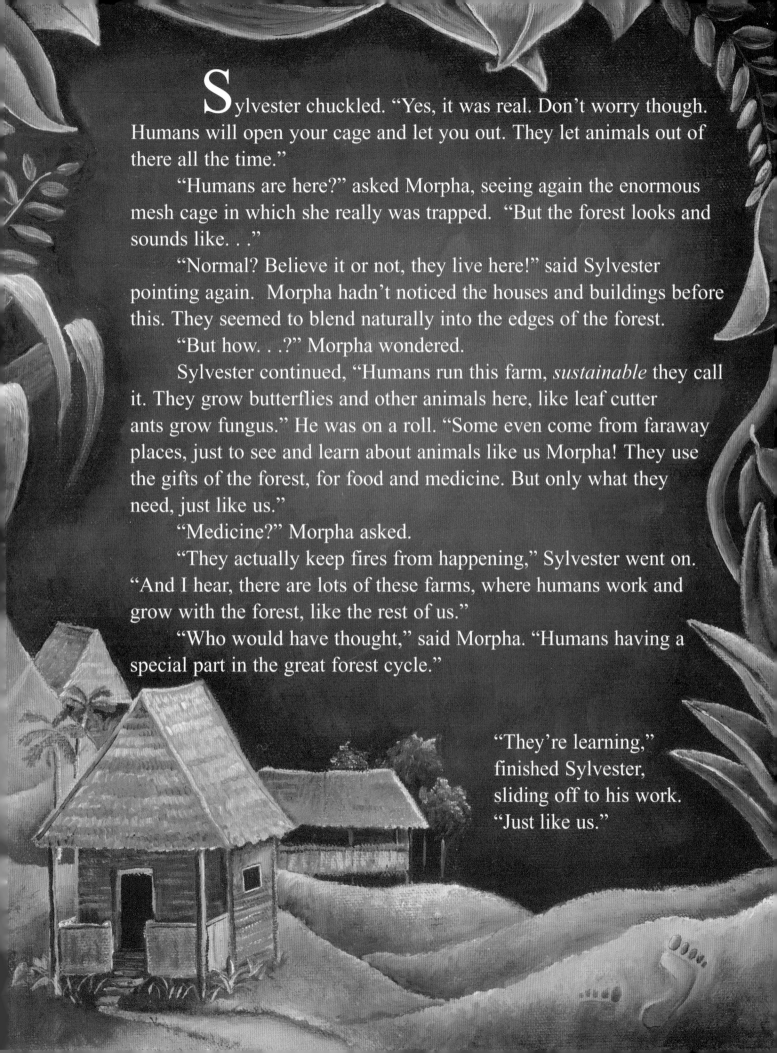

Sylvester chuckled. "Yes, it was real. Don't worry though. Humans will open your cage and let you out. They let animals out of there all the time."

"Humans are here?" asked Morpha, seeing again the enormous mesh cage in which she really was trapped. "But the forest looks and sounds like. . ."

"Normal? Believe it or not, they live here!" said Sylvester pointing again. Morpha hadn't noticed the houses and buildings before this. They seemed to blend naturally into the edges of the forest.

"But how. . .?" Morpha wondered.

Sylvester continued, "Humans run this farm, *sustainable* they call it. They grow butterflies and other animals here, like leaf cutter ants grow fungus." He was on a roll. "Some even come from faraway places, just to see and learn about animals like us Morpha! They use the gifts of the forest, for food and medicine. But only what they need, just like us."

"Medicine?" Morpha asked.

"They actually keep fires from happening," Sylvester went on. "And I hear, there are lots of these farms, where humans work and grow with the forest, like the rest of us."

"Who would have thought," said Morpha. "Humans having a special part in the great forest cycle."

"They're learning," finished Sylvester, sliding off to his work. "Just like us."

Morpha was set free of the cage, just as Sylvester predicted. She came to love these new forest animals. She flitted among Humans, even landing on them, as they all went about their work.

Morpha lived long in the canopy of the forest, just as a proper Blue Morpho should. Touring through the forest floor, she even surprised her old friend Tigerump, brought here to live just as she had been.

Resting her old, weary legs on the leaf of a Mucuna plant, she watched a young butterfly struggle out of its chrysalis. She thought back to the day she had become a butterfly. Fondly, she remembered Azuela, and all her teachings. How much she — and what she thought about the forest — had changed! She knew now she was a part of this new butterfly's life: the sun, the water, and the great cycle of life in the rain forest.

Morpha looked down at the butterfly as it hung exhausted on the branch. It's beautiful, blue wings, slowly expanding, shimmered like a rainbow in the soft morning light.

"Hello little one," Morpha said tenderly. "You have much to learn."

GLOSSARY | *Important terms and names from the story*

abdomen: (AB-duh-min) The largest and rear most segment of an insect's three body parts.

antennae: (an-TEN-ay) The plural of antenna, which are either of a pair of feelers, or sense organs on an insect's head.

Atta ant: (AT-tuh) A species of leafcutter ant found in the Central American rain forest.

Azuela: (ah-ZWAY-la) The older Blue Morpho butterfly who teaches Morpha in the story. Morpha's 'blue grandmother.'

azure: (az-YUR) A color shade blue often referred to as 'sky blue.'

Blue Morpho: (MOR-foh) A species of butterfly with wings of iridescent blue on top and brown with 'eyespots' on the underside. Gets its name because it can change, or 'morph,' its appearance by either opening or closing its wings.

camouflage: (CAM-uf-laj) The coloration of animals' bodies that allows them to blend into their natural surroundings or habitat.

canopy: (KAN-uh-pee) One of the four layers of rainforest stratification. From the bottom are: the forest floor, the under story, the canopy and finally the emergent, or topmost layer.

Cecropia: (suh-KROH-pee-uh) A large rain forest tree with fan-like leaves

chrysalis: (KRIS-uhl-is) The third stage in a butterfly's life cycle, known as the pupae stage.

Cicada: (suh-KAY-dah) A large insect with transparent wings. The male makes a loud trilling sound.

forest floor: (FOR-ist flor) The ground level of tropical rain forest strata. A very low lit, moist environment that provides dead leaves and rotting fruit for ground dwelling animals.

Jacamar: (JAK-uh-mar) A large blue, green and red rain forest bird and a predator of Blue Morpho Butterflies.

Kapok: (KAY-pawk) A giant rain forest tree used for its fibers, among other uses. Sacred among Maya people

liana: (lee-AH-nuh) Thick, woody vines that support themselves on the branches of tall rainforest trees.

Mango: (MANG-go) A tropical tree which produces large green, succulent fruits.

Morada orchid: (mor-AH-duh OR-kid) A beautiful species of rain forest flower. The national flower of Costa Rica.

Papaya: (puh-PIE-yuh) A tropical tree that produces sweet, yellow fibrous fruits.

proboscis: (proh-BOS-is) A long, flexible tube-shaped mouthpart of a butterfly through which it sips its food, and rolls up when not in use.

pupa: (PYOO-puh) The life stage of an insect between its larva (second) and adult (last) stage. Also known as the chrysalis in butterflies.

pupal case: (PYOO-pul kays) See chrysalis. The surrounding structure a butterfly encases itself in during its pupa stage.

sustainable: (suh-STANE-uh-bull) A conservation technique in which only part of a crop or plant is harvested, leaving the rest to grow. This minimizes negative impact on the forest and increases the diversity of native plants and animals.

Tarantula: (tuh-RAN-choo-la) A large, hairy group of spiders that have fangs that bite downward, instead of side to side as other spiders.

under story: (UN-der STOR-ee) From the bottom, the second layer of rain forest strata that includes unique plants and animals.

TEACHER'S HELP PAGE
using this book in the classroom

Azuela advises Morpha that every event is filled with new secrets to learn and pass on. Likewise, all the pages of this book, as well as most specific events in the story, are filled with lessons for use in the classroom or home. The book is aligned for use with numerous education standards in Science, Geography, and Language Arts. Hopefully, the story will encourage education about, and conservation of, the world's remaining tropical rain forests. These lush and fruitful, but quickly vanishing environments, are home to the most diverse populations of plants and animals on Earth, and of vital import to the health of our planet.

LIFE SCIENCE
Life Cycles of Butterflies / Invertebrates
Animal Classification
Habitats
Food Chains and Food Webs
Predator / Prey Relationships
Symbiosis / Co-evolution
Environmental Adaptation: Camouflage and Coloration
Populations and Communities / Diversity

EARTH SCIENCE
Tropical Rain Forest Ecology
The Water Cycle

GEOGRAPHY
Environment
Physical Systems: Ecosystems
Places and Regions: Landforms, Physical and Human characteristics
Human Systems: Cultural Patterns, Economic Interdependence, Human Settlement

LANGUAGE ARTS
Reading: Fiction Genre / Strategies and Skills / Structure / Information Literacy
Writing: Process / Modes and Forms (Expository, Descriptive/Creative,
Persuasive, Narrative)

VISUAL ARTS
Design Elements and Principles: symmetry, pattern, and color theory

This book was made possible by funding provided by the SCIENTIFIC & CULTURAL FACILITIES DISTRICT (SCFD) of Colorado

What is the Scientific & Cultural Facilities District (SCFD)? The *Butterfly Pavilion* and the *Colorado Mountain Club* receive funds collected by the Scientific and Cultural Facilities District. In 1988, greater Denver metropolitan area voters created the Scientific & Cultural Facilities District to provide a consistent source of unrestricted funding to scientific and cultural organizations. Since then, the SCFD has funded over 300 organizations via the 0.1% retail sales and use tax (a penny on every $10). The SCFD facilitates the annual distribution of tax funds to organizations that provide for the enlightenment and entertainment of the public through the production, preservation, exhibition, advancement or preservation of art, music, theater, dance, zoology, botany, natural history or cultural history.

SCFD
Scientific & Cultural Facilities District

Making It Possible.

www.scfd.org

THANK YOU ... to the citizens of Colorado!

The SCFD helps make Colorado a great place to live, work and play. It is the largest citizen-supported cultural initiative in the nation. The district is a jewel that not only supports a better quality of life for our citizens, it is an economic asset that creates jobs, attracts new business and diversifies our economy. It is a remarkable form of self-investment that pays incredible dividends for Colorado.